PAW Patrol is on a roll! Ryder and the pups are heading out of the Lookout to help around Adventure Bay. Can you find each pup?

Zuma

Skye

Rubble

Chase

Everest

Rocky

Marshall

Ready, set, get wet! Zuma races to Cap'n Turbot's boat to patch a leak with a piece of metal he got from Rocky's recyclables. Rocky stays behind—and he stays nice and dry! Find these other animals in the sand, sea, or sky:

seagull

crab

turtle

dolphin

pelican

whale

Farmer Yumi needs a helping hand — or paw — at harvest time! Rubble is ready with his bulldozer. Help him find these fruit patches:

apple

blueberry

strawberry

pear

pumpkin

cherry

Buckle up! It's time for
an Adventure Bay
road race. When Alex
needs help getting his
trike back on the road,
Chase is on the case!
Find these vehicles
behind Chase's
roadblock:

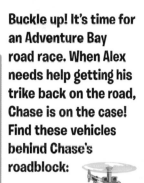
Skye's
copter

Rocky's
recycling truck

Zuma's
hovercraft

Marshall's
fire truck

Everest's
snowcat

Rubble's
digger

Please
DO NOT
LITTER

Uh-oh! Mayor Goodway can't find Chickaletta anywhere! Marshall is all fired up! He climbs his ladder to search the trees. Can you help find Chickaletta and these other birds, too?

pigeon

blue jay

sparrow

rooster

cardinal

Chickaletta

Adventure Bay Snow Day is about to begin! But Jake is stuck on a snowy mountain ledge. Ice or snow, Everest is ready to go! While she uses her pup pack to save the day, find these other things on the mountain:

magnifying glass

flashlight

canteen

compass

map

shovel

Uh-oh! Somehow one of Mr. Porter's birthday cakes got onto the roof of his delivery van. Skye's gotta fly! Search for these tasty treats while Skye takes the cake:

this doughnut

this cupcake

crepe

this pie

this cookie

tart

Who wants to play?
At the end of the day,
the pups love to play
with Ryder at the
Pup Park. Look for
these things the pups
enjoy:

skateboard

jump rope

wagon

tether ball

ball

slide

Don't lose it, reuse it! Find these old things around the Lookout that Rocky can recycle:

old bicycle chain guard

dented pizza pan

banged-up garbage can lid

cracked surfboard

smashed snare drum

broken folding chair

A day at the beach wouldn't be complete without collecting a few seashells! Stay dry with Rocky and find these shells in the sand:

this clam shell

this conch shell

this scallop shell

this nautilus shell

this cowry shell

this sea urchin shell

Farming is a big job that requires lots of tools. Flip back to the farm and find these things Farmer Yumi uses:

barrel

rake

ladder

wheelbarrow

shovel

pitchfork

Caution! Return to the race and find these signs:

start/finish sign

STOP

stop sign

turn ahead sign

race map

CAUTION

caution sign

YIELD

yield sign

Snow way! Make your way back to the mountain and find these snowflakes:

Chickaletta has lots of bird friends in Adventure Bay. Search city hall for these bird eggs:

When the pups save the day, Ryder gives them pup treats to celebrate a job well done. Patrol the Pup Park and find **10** pup treats.

Thanks to the PAW Patrol, Mr. Porter's cakes are safe. Now he needs to bake some more for tomorrow! Trot back to the café and look for these ingredients:

flour

sugar

milk

eggs

sprinkles

chocolate chips